This edition first published in Great Britain in 2017 by
ANDERSEN PRESS LIMITED
20 Vauxhall Bridge Road
London SW1V 2SA
www.andersenpress.co.uk

British Library Cataloguing in
Publication Data available.

ISBN 978 1 78344 572 1

Printed and bound in Turkey by
Omur Printing Co, Istanbul

THE LITTLE BOOK OF SPOOKY JOKES

Illustrated by Nigel Baines

ANDERSEN PRESS

GHOSTLY GAGS

What is a little ghost's favourite game?

Peek-a-boo

What is a ghost's favourite party game?

Hide-and-shriek

How do ghosts fall in love?

It's love at first fright

What story do little ghosts like to hear at bedtime?

Ghouldelocks and the Three Scares

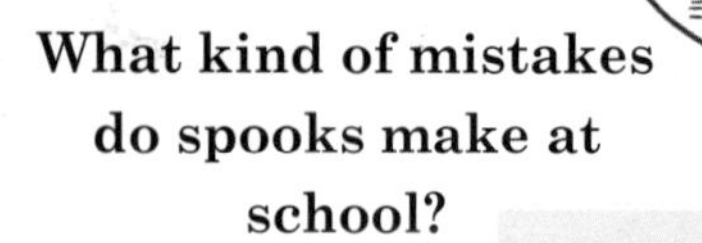

What kind of mistakes do spooks make at school?

Boo-boos

What did the ghost teacher say to her class?

'Watch the board and I'll go through it again!'

Why was the young ghost's birthday party so noisy?

His friends gave him the bumps in the night

What do ghosts eat for dinner?

Spook-ghetti

What is a ghost's favourite dessert?

Boo-berry pie with I-scream

How do ghosts check that their paintings hang straight?

With a spirit level

What do you call a ghost with an upset stomach?

Spew-ky

What did the polite ghost say to her son?

'Don't spook until you're spooken to!'

Where do ghosts post their letters?

At the ghost office

What do you call a prehistoric ghost?

A terror-dactyl

Why are ghosts bad at telling lies?

Because you can see right through them

Who was the famous ghost detective?

Sherlock Moans

Did you hear about the deceased comedian?

He was dead funny

How can you tell when a ghost is scared?

He goes as white as a sheet

Where do ghosts swim?

The Dead Sea

What is a ghost's favourite bird?

A scare crow

What happens when a ghost gets lost in the fog?

He is mist

What do short-sighted ghosts wear?
Spooktacles

MONSTER MAYHEM

What's the best way to speak to a monster?

From a long way away

What do you say to a monster with a dribbly nose?

'Goo away!'

How did the Hunchback of Notre Dame cure his sore throat?

He gargoyled

What is the Loch Ness Monster's favourite takeaway meal?
Fish 'n' ships

Where do zombies go on holiday?

The Deaditerranean

Where does the monster keep his hands?

In a hand bag

What happens when an ogre sits in front of you at the cinema?

You miss most of the film

Who won the ogres' beauty contest?

No one

What do you call someone who likes to pick his nose under the bed?
The Bogeyman

What happened at the monsters' wedding party?

They toasted the bride and groom

What did the monster say when he was full?

'I couldn't eat another mortal!'

Why don't monsters eat weather forecasters?
Because they give them wind

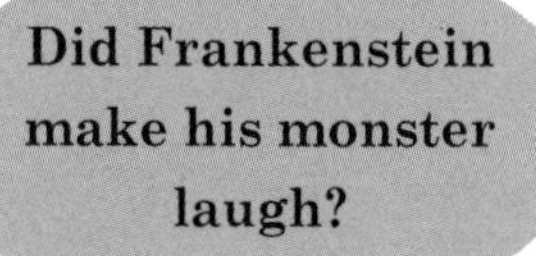

Yes, he kept him in stitches

How do monsters cook their food?

They terror-fry it

What do mummies do on the weekends?

They unwind

Why couldn't the mummy answer the phone?

Because it was all tied up

What do ghosts say when something is really great?

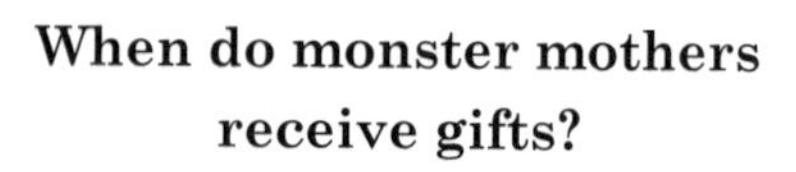

On mummy's day

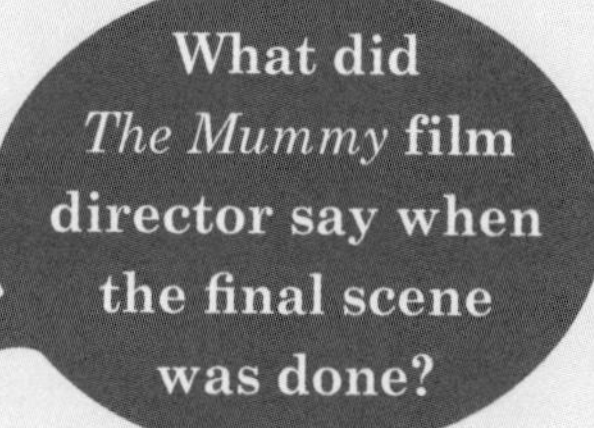

'OK, that's a wrap!'

How do you open a haunted house?

With a skeleton key

Why was Frankenstein's monster late for the party?

He couldn't pull himself together in time

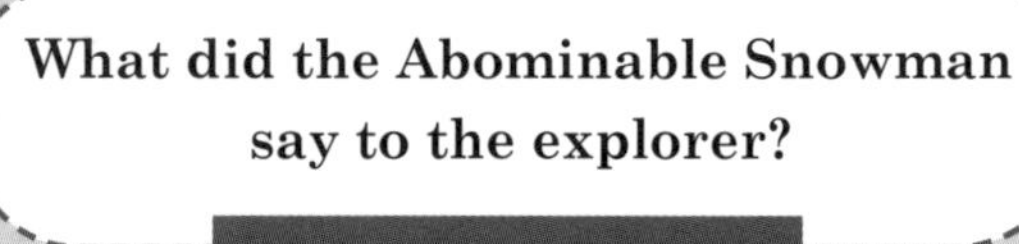

'Nice to meat you!'

What would you do if you opened the front door and saw Dracula, Frankenstein's monster, three ghosts, a werewolf and eight witches standing on the doorstep?

Hope it was Halloween

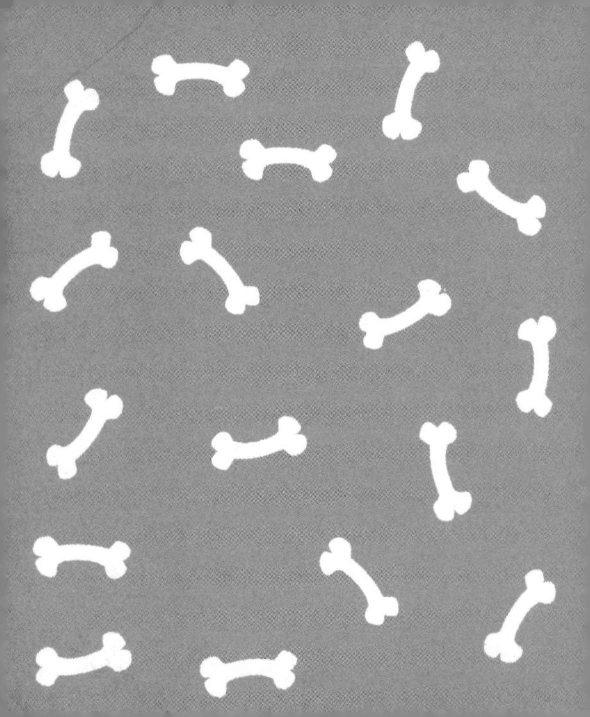

SKELETON SCREAMERS

What type of art do skeletons like?
Skull-tures

When does a skeleton laugh?

When someone tickles its funny bone

What did the skeleton say
while riding his Harley-
Davidson motorcycle?
'I'm bone to be wild!'

What instrument do skeletons play?

Trom-bone

Who was the most famous French skeleton?

Napoleon Bone-Apart

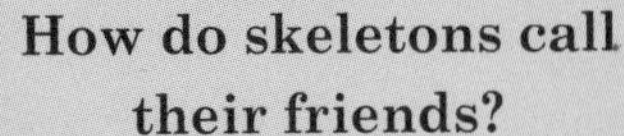

On the telebone

Why didn't the skeleton play church music?

He had no organs

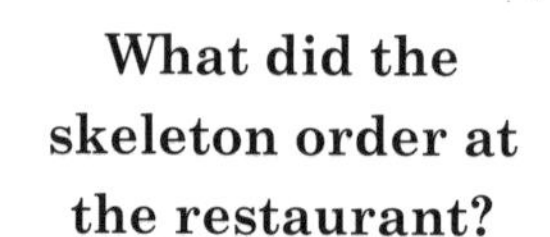

What did the skeleton order at the restaurant?

Spare ribs

What do you call a skeleton who won't get up in the morning?

Lazy bones

Why didn't the skeleton want to play football?

Because his heart wasn't in it

How did the skeleton know it was going to rain?

He could feel it in his bones

Why are skeletons so lazy?

They're bone idle

What do skeletons say before they begin dining?
'Bone appétit!'

Why didn't the skeleton cross the road?

He didn't have the guts

FANGTASTIC VAMPIRE JOKES

What did the teacher say to Dracula after he failed his maths test?

'Can't you count, Dracula?'

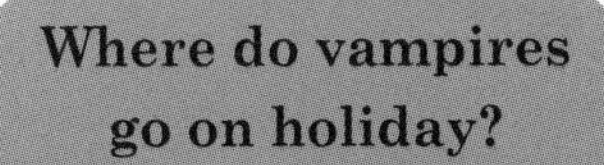

Where do vampires go on holiday?

The Isle of Fright

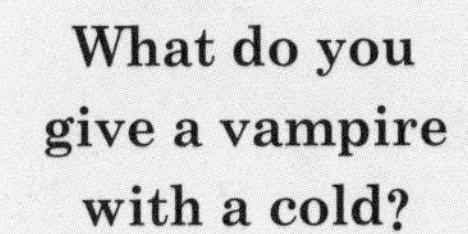

What do you give a vampire with a cold?

Coffin drops

What kind of ship does Dracula own?

Who plays centre forward for the vampire football team?

Knock, knock

Who's there?

Discount

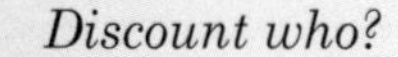

Discount who?

Discount is named Dracula

What do you get if you cross Dracula with Al Capone?

A fangster

Why does Dracula brush his teeth after every meal?
To avoid bat-breath

Why doesn't Dracula give up being a vampire?

He can't, it's in his

BLOOD

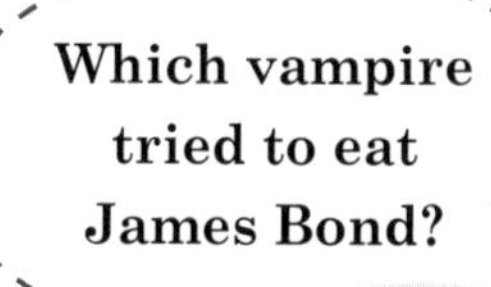

Ghouldfinger

What flavour ice cream is Dracula's favourite?

Veinilla

What happened when the vampire began to write poetry?

He went from bat to verse

Why should you avoid vampires at dawn?

Because they like a quick bite before they go to bed

Where does Dracula do most of his singing?

In the bat-tub

What would you get if you crossed a vampire bat and a magician?

A flying sorcerer

Why doesn't Dracula mind the doctor looking at his throat?

Because of the coffin

Why is Dracula able to live so cheaply?

He lives on necks to nothing

Where do vampires keep their savings?

IN A BLOOD BANK

How does Dracula play cricket?

With a vampire bat

What do you call a vampire who likes to relax in a bloodbath with a good book?

Well red

The door is stuck, you'll have to come in through the bat-flap!

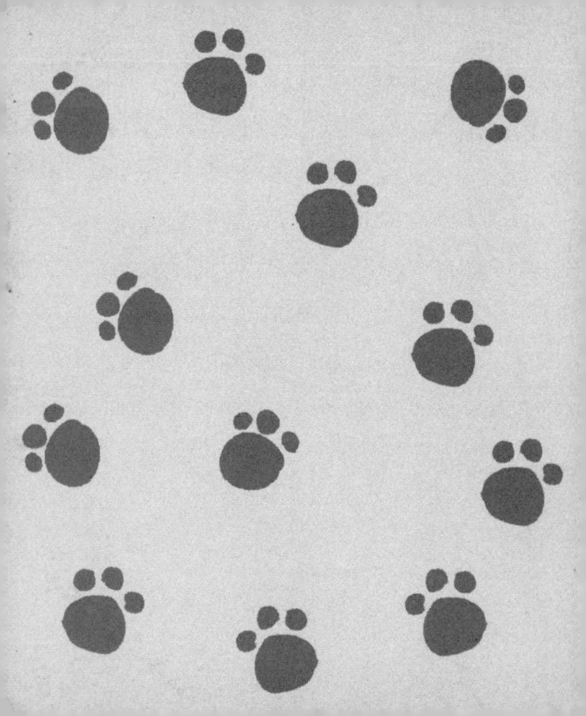

WEREWOLF
HOWLERS

What happened when the werewolf chewed a bone for an hour?

When he got up he only had three legs

How do you make a werewolf stew?

Keep him waiting for two hours

What kind of beans do werewolves like?

Human beans

What is fearsome, hairy and drinks from the wrong side of a glass?

A werewolf with hiccups

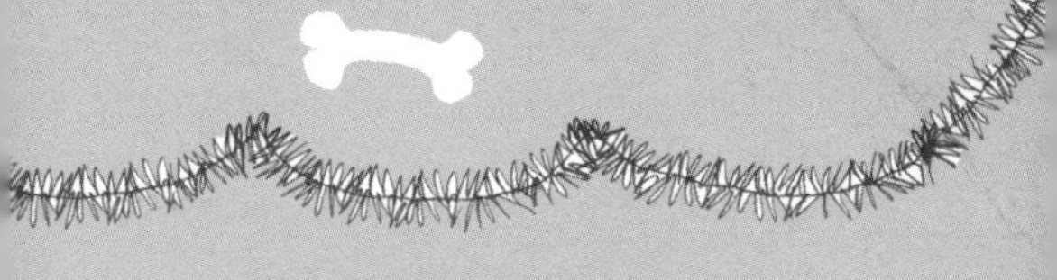

How was the werewolf's birthday party?

It was a howling success

What happens if you cross a werewolf and a sheep?

You have to get a new sheep

William: Mum, all the children make fun of me.

Mum: What do they say?

William: They say I'm a werewolf. Is it true?

Mum: Of course not. Now comb your face and get ready for supper.

Why does the werewolf sleep all day long?

Who wants to wake him up?

What kind of fur do you get from a werewolf?

As fur as you can

What happened when the werewolf swallowed a clock?

He got ticks

Which scary creature is always getting lost?

A where-wolf

What type of markets do werewolves go to?

Flea markets

Why do werewolves do well at school?

Because every time they're asked a question, they give a snappy answer

Why did the werewolf finally take a bath?
He decided to give up his life of grime

WITCH CACKLERS

What is a witch's favourite subject at school?

Spelling

What does a witch ask for when she is in a hotel?
Broom service

Why do witches wear nametags?

So they know which witch is which

MAGIC!
What noise does a witch's breakfast cereal make?
Snap, cackle and pop
AS SEEN IN WITCH MAGAZINE
SNAP
CACKLE

What do you get if you cross a witch and an iceberg?

A cold spell

How does a witch travel when she doesn't have a broom?

She witch-hikes

What do you call two witches living together?

Broom mates

What do you call a witch with one leg?

Eileen

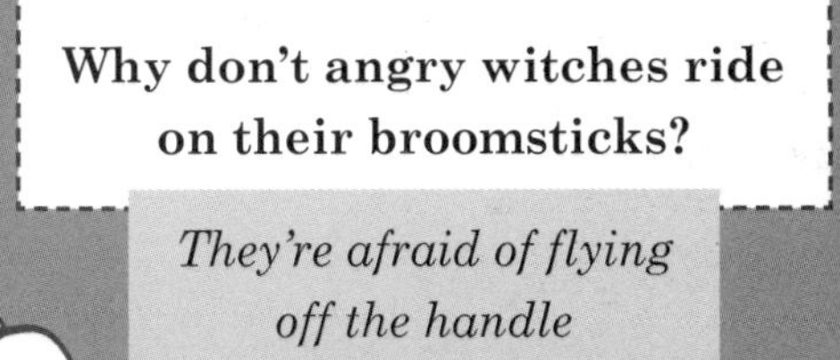

Why don't angry witches ride on their broomsticks?

They're afraid of flying off the handle

What is the difference between a musician and a dead witch?
One composes and the other decomposes

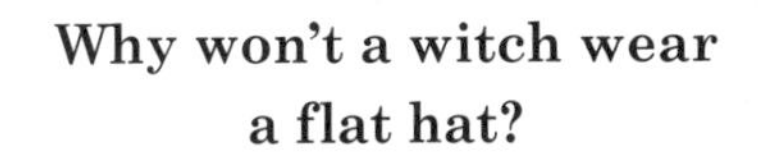

Because there is no point in it

What goes cackle, cackle, bonk?

A witch laughing her head off

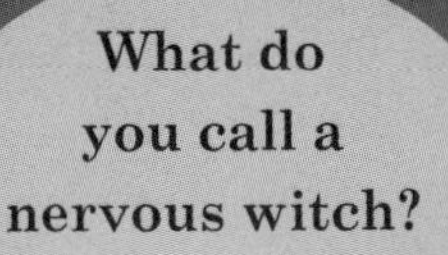

A twitch

What kind of tests do they set at witch school?

Hex-aminations

What happened to the naughty little witch at school?

She was ex-spelled

Why didn't the witch sing at the concert?
Because she had a frog in her throat

Why should men beware of beautiful witches?

They'll sweep them off their feet

What do you get if you cross a dinosaur with a wizard?

Tyrannosaurus hex

What do witches read in the newspaper?

Their horrorscopes

What happened to the wizard who ran away with the circus?

The police made him bring it back again

Witch 1: Are you really going to meet that vampire?

Witch 2: I was, but I'm beginning to have grave doubts.

Witch: Do you want to go dancing tonight?

Zombie: Not tonight, I'm dead on my feet

What do witches put on their hair?

Scare-spray

GRAVESTONE
GAGS

Here lies old
Maud Gaunt.
Not quite
dead, but ready
to haunt.

RIP
Angus Drew.
Died of shock.
Now just
says, 'Boo!'

By day
here lies
Vampire Deck.
If you're reading
this at night,
watch your neck.

Here lies
merry
Terry Bones.
Moody in life,
now emits
loud groans.

RIP
Professor
Rachel Ghoul.
A teacher in life,
now teaches
ghoul school.

Here lies
smelly Kelly.
Silent but deadly.

RIP
Jumping
Jack Dean.
Rotten, scary
ugly and mean.
Oh he's behind
you, don't scream!

Here lies
Hypochondriac
Bill.
'I told you
I was ill!'

HAPPY
HALLOWEEN!

Collect them all!

The Funniest Animal Joke Book Ever

The Funniest Back to School Joke Book Ever

The Funniest Christmas Joke Book Ever

The Funniest Dinosaur Joke Book Ever

The Funniest Football Joke Book Ever

The Funniest Holiday Joke Book Ever

The Funniest Space Joke Book Ever